Monica

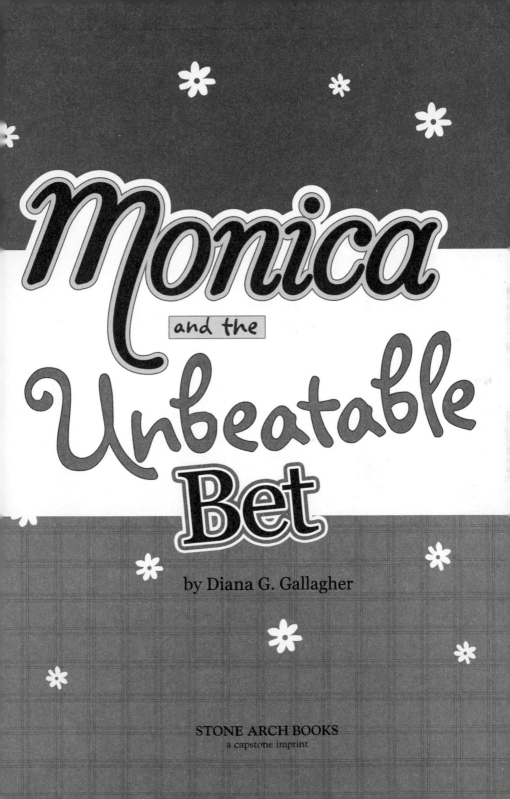

and the

Unbeatable

Bet

by Diana G. Gallagher

STONE ARCH BOOKS
a capstone imprint

Monica is published by Stone Arch Books
A Capstone Imprint
151 Good Counsel Drive, P.O. Box 669
Mankato, Minnesota 56002
www.capstonepub.com

Printed in the United States of America in Stevens Point, Wisconsin.
032011
006111WZF11

Library of Congress Cataloging-in-Publication Data
Gallagher, Diana G.
  Monica and the unbeatable bet / by Diana G. Gallagher.
    p. cm.
  Summary: Monica is already nervous about riding in her first horse show, and when she finds out that Rory is betting on her performance it only increases the pressure she feels.
  ISBN-13: 978-1-4342-2555-9 (library binding)
  ISBN-10: 1-4342-2555-0 (library binding)
  1. Horse shows--Competitions--Juvenile fiction. 2. Competition (Psychology)--Juvenile fiction. 3. Wagers--Juvenile fiction. 4. Worry--Juvenile fiction. 5. Interpersonal relations--Juvenile fiction. [1. Horse shows--Fiction. 2. Competition (Psychology)--Fiction. 3. Wagers--Fiction. 4. Worry--Fiction. 5. Interpersonal relations--Fiction.] I. Title.
  PZ7.G13543Mpo 2011
  813.54--dc22
                              2011001995

Art Director/Graphic Designer: Kay Fraser
Production Specialist: Michelle Biedscheid

Photo credits:
Cover: Delaney Photography
Avatars: Delaney Photography (Claudia), Shutterstock: Aija Avotina (guitar), Alex Staroseltsev (baseball), Andrii Muzyka (bowling ball), Anton9 (reptile), bsites (hat), debra hughes (tree), Dietmar Höpfl (lightning), Dr_Flash (Earth), Elaine Barker (star), Ivelin Radkov (money), Michael D Brown (smiley face), Mikhail (horse), originalpunkt (paintbrushes), pixel-pets (dog), R. Gino Santa Maria (football), Ruth Black (cupcake), Shvaygert Ekaterina (horseshoe), SPYDER (crown), Tischenko Irina (flower), VectorZilla (clown), Volkova Anna (heart); Capstone Studio: Karon Dubke (horse Monica, horse Chloe)

---------------------{ table of contents }---------------------

WELCOME BACK, MONICA MURRAY   SCREEN NAME: MonicaLuvsHorses

 YOUR AVATAR PICTURE

All updates from your friends

 MARK BRISTOW has invited you to an event: Practice Horse Show at Rock Creek Stables. Your current RSVP status is: Yes
> Rory Weber and 2 other people like this.

 CLAUDIA CORTEZ to BECCA MCDOUGAL Want to see a movie on Wednesday night?

> BECCA MCDOUGAL Yes! Let's invite Monica, too.

> CLAUDIA CORTEZ Okay, I'll text her.

 RORY WEBER Can't wait for the practice show. There's nothing I like more than a horse show. This weekend will be really fun!
> You and 3 other people like this.   Unlike

> MONICA MURRAY I am so nervous!

> RORY WEBER   Don't be. You're going to be great.

> CHLOE GRANGER Nervousness is WHY Mark has these practice shows, silly!

> MONICA MURRAY I know. But still.

> MARK BRISTOW   I'm not worried, Monica. Why would you be?

 MEGAN FITCH may have to spend Saturday at a fake horse show for babies, but I'll be riding in style this weekend. Thanks for the brand new riding gear, Mom and Dad!

BECCA MCDOUGAL has updated her information. She added "Painting portraits" to her interests.

 OWEN HARGROVE III to MEGAN FITCH I can't believe we have to waste a whole Saturday at the practice show.

> MEGAN FITCH   I know. What a waste of time for those of us who actually know what we're doing!

> MARK BRISTOW   You know I can read this, right?

 CHLOE GRANGER I'm loading up on protein and stocking up on sunscreen before the big practice show this Saturday. What's your favorite way to get energy?

> RORY WEBER   Energy drinks!

> MONICA MURRAY   Sleeping in late.

> OWEN HARGROVE III   Spending money.

> MEGAN FITCH   Winning.

 MEGAN FITCH is thinking about when I won my very first riding competition. Ahhhh...memories!
>   Owen Hargrove III likes this

Messages to MonicaLuvsHorses

ClaudiaCristina said:
Becca and I are going to the movies. Want to come?

MonicaLuvsHorses said:
I'd love to, but I can't. Horse stuff.

Chapter One

Practice Makes
Perfect?

Chloe and I were happy when Mark Bristow, the trainer at our stable, decided to have a practice horse show.

It had been months since the last show. Chloe wanted a warm-up. I wanted the experience.

Owen, Megan, and Lydia thought it was a stupid idea. And they made that very clear on Wednesday after our lesson while we brushed down our horses in the stable. They just kept whining and complaining about spending a whole Saturday at the barn.

"This is really unfair," Megan said. "We should each get to choose whether we want to do this practice show or not."

"Mark wants everyone to do well at Holly Hills in two weeks," Alice explained. "This is a perfect way to practice."

The Holly Hills Horse Show was the first real show of the season. It was a huge event.

"I've been in lots of horse shows," Owen said. "I know what to do."

"I don't," I said, shrugging. "Holly Hills is my first show."

"It's the first show for three other students, too," Alice added.

"That's not my problem," Megan said. She scowled at me.

"It's Mark's problem, Megan," Rory said. He leaned on his pitchfork. "He wants everyone to do well, and for the stable to look good. You don't want to let Mark down, do you?"

"No, of course not," Megan said. She sighed and glared at me again.

"I already have other plans for Saturday!" Lydia whined.

Alice shrugged. "If you want to show at Holly Hills, you have to practice this Saturday," she said. "That's it. Mark sets the rules, and you guys all know that. **This practice show is really important to him.** So if it's important to you, you'll be here." Then she turned around and walked out of the stable.

"Maybe that is a good idea," Owen said. "Mark will find out which lesson kids are good enough to enter Holly Hills."

"Yeah," Megan said. Then she looked me right in the eye and added, "And it'll help him find out who isn't good enough."

I blinked. "Does that mean if I mess up Mark won't let me show?" I asked. I looked over at Chloe, hoping she could make me feel better.

"No," Megan said. "It means that if you mess up at the dumb practice show, you might realize you shouldn't be riding in the first place."

* * *

Messages to Horses4Chloe

MonicaLuvsHorses said:
I'm really, really nervous about Saturday.

Horses4Chloe said:
Don't worry! Everyone gets horse show jitters.

Horses4Chloe said:
You're going to be fine.

MonicaLuvsHorses said:
I won't look fine, Chloe. I don't have a hunt coat OR a velvet helmet. I'm going to look like an idiot.

Horses4Chloe said:
You don't need formal gear to practice. Stop worrying!

MonicaLuvsHorses said:
Okay, I'll try. Thanks, Chloe. :)

All the show riders met at the barn Friday afternoon.

"We're going to prep like tomorrow is a real show," Mark said. "Bathe and braid your horses, and don't forget to clean your tack."

Lydia made a face. "Saddle soap dries out my hands," she complained.

"There's lotion in the tack room," Chloe said.

"Rory always gets Dandy ready for me," Megan whined.

"Rory is setting up the show ring," Mark said.

I saw Rory loading jump poles onto a flatbed trailer. That was hard work, but it was better than being bossed around by spoiled stable brats.

"Let's team up, Monica," Chloe said. "You can hold Rick-Rack while I wash him. Then I'll hold Lancelot for you."

"Good plan!" I said. I led Rick-Rack outside.

The other students groomed the lesson horses in the small barn. The kids who owned their own horses were cleaning saddles and bridles. That meant we didn't have to wait for the hose.

Rick-Rack stood still while Chloe wet his coat. She lathered him with soap, and then rinsed it all off. Then she cleaned the dirt out of his hooves.

"I can feel the excitement in the air! Is that weird?" I asked.

"It's anticipation,"

Chloe said. "Everyone feels it the day before a horse show."

Lancelot did not like his bath. He pranced, shook his head, and swished his tail. Soon, he was clean, but I was covered with soapy smears and dirt spatters.

Chloe and I thought it was funny. I didn't mind getting a little dirty — or soapy.

As soon as Megan walked out of the barn, she started laughing. Rory was walking behind her, leading Dandy. He smiled at me.

"Monica lost a water fight with a horse!" Megan yelled, laughing.

I felt my face get hot, but Rory didn't seem to care that I was all wet and muddy. After all, he was dirty too. It was part of the job.

"Lancelot looks great, Monica," Rory said. "He's hard to wash when he won't stand still. You did a really good job."

Megan frowned. I hurried inside before she had time to insult me again.

I put Lancelot in his stall. Chloe tied Rick-Rack in the center aisle.

Messages to Guitar_Rory, Horses4Chloe, MonicaLuvsHorses, Pretty_Megan, OwenIII

MarkRockCreekStables said:
Don't forget to braid your horses' manes.

"I'm terrible at this," I said, gazing at Lancelot's deep brown mane.

"Braiding isn't hard," Chloe said. "It just takes practice."

Show-horse braids looked like little nubs on the horse's neck. Chloe showed me how to do it.

You take a small lock of mane, braid it, tuck the end under, and then hold it with a rubber band.

Chloe's braids were neat, small, and evenly spaced. Mine were too big or too small with flyaway hairs. They weren't evenly spaced, and they didn't lie flat.

"That's the worst braiding job I've ever seen!" Megan exclaimed when she saw it.

I didn't argue. She was right.

"Why does she pick on me so much?" I asked Chloe once Megan flounced away.

Chloe smiled. "Because she likes Rory, silly," she said. "And she knows Rory likes you."

I understood why Megan liked Rory.

Who wouldn't? He was nice, super cute, and he was fourteen. He also knew a lot about horses. That was a huge plus for me.

I didn't believe he really liked me, no matter what Chloe said. I didn't want to let myself believe it. I didn't want a broken heart like some girls at school.

Boys could be really confusing. One day they liked you. The next day they'd rather hang out with their friends. Or they found someone they liked better.

I was sure Rory wasn't like that. But why risk ruining our friendship?

Chapter Two

Practice
Show

Messages to MonicaLuvsHorses

Horses4Chloe said:
Admit it. You're excited about today.

MonicaLuvsHorses said:
Okay, I admit it, I am! I can't wait!

MonicaLuvsHorses said:
But I'm nervous at the same time.

Horses4Chloe said:
Sounds normal to me. See you soon!

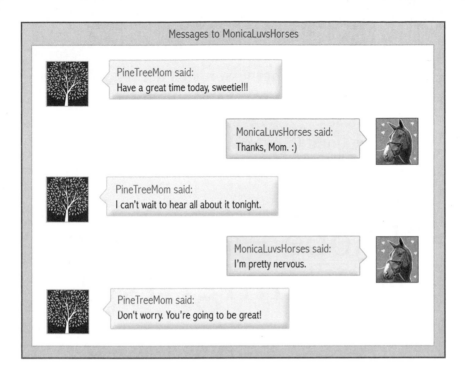

I was thrilled and terrified when I got to the barn on Saturday morning.

This was my only chance to practice for a real horse show.

In my dreams, I beat Megan.

In my nightmares, I fell off!

I'd be happy if I didn't make a major mistake.

Alice helped the other lesson kids get ready. Chloe helped me.

"After we hand in our entry forms, we'll saddle Rick-Rack and Lancelot," Chloe said. "Then we'll warm up and wait for the first class."

"I hope I remember everything," I said.

"You'll be fine. It's just like your riding lesson," Chloe said.

"Yeah, but Megan isn't in my riding lesson," I reminded her.

In real horse shows, beginners and advanced riders entered different classes. Today, we were riding together.

"I've never had butterflies this bad," I told Chloe.

"They'll stop when you get into the ring," Chloe said.

I clutched my stomach. "If they don't, I'll throw up," I muttered.

Then I heard Rory laugh. "You won't throw up," he said.

I felt my face getting hot as I turned around, but as soon as I saw Rory, I forgot about being embarrassed.

He looked so cute. He was wearing a white shirt, britches, and tall boots.

"Look at you! You look so fancy," I said. "Are you riding in a class?"

Rory shook his head. "No," he said. "I'm the ringmaster and half of the jump crew."

"Who's the other half of the jump crew?" Chloe asked.

"Mark," Rory said. "He's also the judge. Megan's mom is taking entries." He pointed to Mrs. Fitch, sitting at a table under a big umbrella.

"What does the jump crew do?" I asked. I felt kind of stupid for not knowing, but I knew that Rory and Chloe wouldn't make fun of me.

"We set up the jumps and take them down, basically," Rory said. "You guys better hurry up," he added. He winked at me and said, "Good luck."

"Thanks," I said.

Chloe nudged me as we walked away.

"True love," she said.

I just laughed.

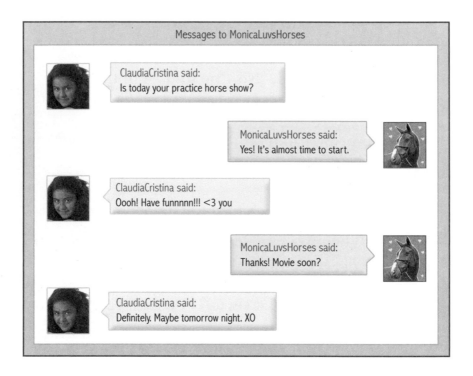

Messages to MonicaLuvsHorses

ClaudiaCristina said:
Is today your practice horse show?

MonicaLuvsHorses said:
Yes! It's almost time to start.

ClaudiaCristina said:
Oooh! Have funnnnn!!! <3 you

MonicaLuvsHorses said:
Thanks! Movie soon?

ClaudiaCristina said:
Definitely. Maybe tomorrow night. XO

Mrs. Fitch smiled when Chloe and I walked up to the sign-in table.

"Hello, girls," she said. "You'll just need to fill this out." She gave each of us a form.

The form asked which classes we'd be riding in.

There were six classes. Field Hunter and Junior Jumper for advanced riders only, Maiden Equitation on the flat and over fences, and Green Hunter Hack and over fences for everyone.

"What do maiden and green mean?" I asked.

"Maiden equitation is for riders who haven't won more than three blue ribbons," Chloe explained.

"A horse is green during its first two years of showing," Mrs. Fitch added.

"So which ones am I?" I asked.

"You'll be in the maiden and green classes at Holly Hills," Chloe told me.

"What?" Megan exclaimed behind me. "Monica can't show Lancelot in green hunter classes."

"Why not?" Megan's mother asked.

"My mom bought Lancelot five years ago," Chloe said. "She's never shown him."

"But he was a show horse before that," Megan said, putting her nose in the air.

"Was he?" I asked, looking at Chloe.

"It doesn't matter," Mrs. Fitch said. "Every horse is green today. Just fill out your form, Monica."

I picked up the pen, but Megan had to have the last word.

"You have to prove Lancelot is a beginner before Holly Hills," she whispered. "Otherwise, he'll be disqualified. And you'll embarrass Mark and the whole barn."

After I finished my entry form, we found Rory in the barn. Chloe told him what had happened.

"Why does Megan care?" Rory asked, frowning.

Chloe and I just shrugged. Neither of us wanted to tell him that she always picked on me because she was jealous that Rory might like me.

"Megan really messed things up," Rory told me. "Now no one will believe Lancelot is a green show horse."

"You could ride him in the Junior Hunter classes," Chloe suggested. "But the jumps are six inches higher."

"There's no way I'm ready for that," I said. "I haven't even been in one show yet!"

Rory nodded. "Then there's only one thing to do," he said. "We have to prove that Lancelot wasn't a show horse before Chloe's mom bought him."

Chloe looked worried. She added, "And we only have two weeks."

Chapter Three

In the
Ring

I knew that Rory and Chloe were on my side. That helped me calm down. The butterflies were gone by the time Chloe and I left the barn a few minutes later.

Rory left before we did. I knew he had a lot to do to get everything ready for the show.

Owen, Lydia, and Megan stopped us as we walked out.

"What did you tell Rory?" Megan asked, glaring at me. "He's mad at me! He wouldn't even talk to me just now."

Chloe crossed her arms. "Monica didn't say anything. I told Rory that you were making trouble," she said.

"Megan's the good guy," Lydia said.

"Horse shows have rules for a reason," Owen said.

Megan nodded. "It's cheating to ride an experienced horse in beginner classes," she told Chloe. "I want Holly Hills to be fair."

Then the three of them walked away.

"Megan is trying to make you nervous," Chloe said. "Just ignore her."

"Yeah, I know," I said. I smiled and nodded, but the butterflies were back.

We headed straight for the warm-up ring and got on our horses.

Rick-Rack was calm. But Lancelot pulled on the bit and tossed his head. Horses could always tell when a rider was nervous.

"Let's wait in the shade," Chloe suggested. "Lancelot will settle down when you relax."

I couldn't relax. Lancelot pawed the ground, snorting and jiggling, until Rory called the first class.

I followed Chloe into the ring. Then my mind went blank. As soon as the gate closed, I forgot everything Alice had taught me.

Like my **diagonals**. When trotting in a circle, the rider rises up off the saddle when the horse's outside leg moves forward.

I didn't look. I just started posting and got it wrong. Mark saw the mistake.

And **leads!** When cantering in a circle, the horse's inside legs should extend farther than its outside legs. Lancelot never took off on the wrong lead.

Until today. Today, Lancelot took the wrong lead. Twice.

"Reverse, please!" Rory shouted.

I turned Lancelot toward the fence.

Everyone else turned into the center.

Everyone else did it right.

At the end of the class, we lined up in the center of the ring. Mark didn't announce winners. He let the advanced kids leave. Then he took each of the beginners aside one by one to tell us how we'd done.

When it was my turn, I looked over at Rory. He gave me a thumbs-up.

"Okay, Monica," Mark said, looking at his notepad. He paused for a while, thinking. Finally, he said, "You made quite a few mistakes."

My heart sank, even though I knew he was right.

"Watch those diagonals and leads," Mark said. He patted me on the back. Then he smiled and added, "Don't worry. I'm sure you'll do better next time. You'll be great at Holly Hills."

I nodded. "Thanks, Mark," I said. "I promise I'll do better next time."

Rory ran over when I walked out the gate.

"I'm so embarrassed," I said.

"Don't be," Rory said. "It was your first time. For the next class, if you're not sure what to do, just watch the other riders."

"Now you tell me!" I joked.

The Hunter Hack class was next. Lancelot acted like a wild mustang. He pranced when he was supposed to walk. He trotted with his nose in the air. He bucked when he cantered.

Afterward, Mark was very disappointed. "A hunter is supposed to be quiet, calm, and easy to ride," he explained. "Lancelot failed all three."

I was mortified.

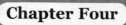
Not
Perfect

Everyone took a break while Mark and Rory set up the jumps. Chloe and I got off our horses. I let Lancelot graze. I wanted him to chill out. I didn't care if he had a green mouth from eating grass.

Megan and Lydia walked by. "You should skip the jumping classes, Monica," Lydia said.

"Yeah. It would be so embarrassing if you fell off," Megan said. She laughed.

Chloe glared at them. I tried to just ignore them. I couldn't back out. I had to prove I could do it.

"Equitation over fences!" Rory shouted. "Owen, you're first! Megan, you're on deck."

Everyone else waited near the gate. I watched Owen and took mental notes.

There were two jumps on each side of the ring. They were two feet high.

First, Owen cantered Merlin around in a small circle. He jumped all the fences twice and walked out of the ring.

"That was perfect, Owen!" Lydia gushed.

Owen rolled his eyes. **"Whatever. Those are baby jumps,"** he said. "Anyone could do them." Then he glanced at me and added, "Well, almost anyone."

Megan had a perfect run too. So did Chloe.

Hanna, one of the lesson kids, rode right before me. She flopped back in the saddle over every fence, but she got around.

Then it was my turn.

"This should be good," Megan said as I walked into the ring. She must have jinxed me. Because starting then, everything went wrong.

First my hands started sweating. I forgot to shorten my reins, and Lancelot cantered too fast. He flew over the first jump. I almost lost a stirrup, and I flopped back in the saddle.

Then Lancelot stopped dead at the second fence. I backed up and trotted over the jump.

I trotted over the third and fourth jumps, too. I hit the saddle hard on both landings.

Lancelot didn't like that at all. He stopped at the fifth fence. I fell forward on his neck. I scooted back into the saddle and tried it again.

Lancelot didn't stop this time. He ran around the jump.

I heard a loud horn.

"Three refusals," Rory yelled. "The rider is excused." I looked over at him, but he didn't look back at me. I felt horrible.

As soon as I dismounted, I found Chloe. "I'm not going in the next class," I told her.

Chloe gasped. "You can't quit now," she said.

"Lancelot is acting up because I'm a bad rider," I said. "I don't want to ruin your mother's horse."

Chloe laughed. "You aren't going to ruin him," she said. "You should see the way my dad rides." She waved her arms around and pretended to bounce up and down on a horse. "Seriously, if my father can ride Lancelot and not ruin him forever," Chloe said, "I think you'll be fine."

I laughed. "Maybe you're right," I said. "But still. I don't want to look stupid."

"Just get around the course," Chloe said.

"Even if I have to walk it?" I asked.

"Whatever it takes," Chloe said.

"Okay," I said.

I trotted over eight fences in the next course, but I was still disqualified.

That's because I forgot about the ninth fence in the middle.

"Everybody goes off course sometimes," Chloe said afterward.

"Yeah," I said. "I know."

I wasn't that upset about being disqualified again. I had gotten around most of the fences, and Lancelot hadn't refused. At least it was better than the last time.

"That was better than my first jumping class," Rory said, walking over to us. "I fell off. Twice."

"Weren't you embarrassed?" I asked.

"Yep." Rory laughed. "But I took a bow, got back on, and tried again. Everyone cheered when I finished." He checked his watch. "You better hurry, Chloe," he said. "The advanced classes are going to start soon."

"Good luck," I told her. Then I headed back to the barn with Lancelot. But as I walked, Megan ambushed me.

"You can't ride at Holly Hills," she told me. "Seriously, Monica. This is a big deal."

"Why?" I asked, turning to face her.

She shook her head. "Don't you get it?" she said. "You're terrible. You're so bad you'll hurt Mark's reputation. Do you really want to make him look bad? Because that's what you'll do if you ride at Holly Hills."

That's when I made a decision.

I couldn't hurt Mark.

And that meant I couldn't ride in the show at Holly Hills.

Chapter Five

Words of
Wisdom

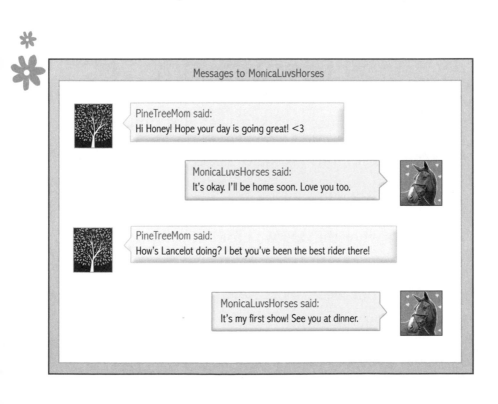

Messages to MonicaLuvsHorses

PineTreeMom said:
Hi Honey! Hope your day is going great! <3

MonicaLuvsHorses said:
It's okay. I'll be home soon. Love you too.

PineTreeMom said:
How's Lancelot doing? I bet you've been the best rider there!

MonicaLuvsHorses said:
It's my first show! See you at dinner.

That night at dinner, the last thing I wanted to do was talk about the horse show.

As soon as Logan sat down, he smiled at me. "Tell us all about the horse show," he said.

Everyone at the dinner table looked at me.

Mom handed me a plate of rolls. "I bet you're starving!" she said. "You probably got a lot of exercise today."

Actually, I was feeling sick to my stomach. But I had to tell them something about my day.

"I did okay, since it was just my first time," I said.

"Did you fall off?" Angela asked.

"No," I said. "But I missed a jump."

"That's what the day was for," Grandpa said. "That's why Mark wanted you to practice before Holly Hills. To see where your weak spots were and figure out a way to fix any problems. Right?"

I just nodded.

I knew I wasn't going to show at Holly Hills, but I didn't want to tell them yet. I forced myself to eat, because I knew I'd need the energy — and I had gotten a lot of exercise.

But eating the rolls was like chewing cardboard, and the chicken made me feel sick.

After dinner, Mom went into the kitchen. She came back with three wrapped boxes. She handed them all to me.

"Hey!" Angela yelled. "Don't I get a present?"

"Not today," Logan said.

Angela frowned and folded her arms. "It's not her birthday," she said.

"Nope, it's not," Mom said. "And sometimes you get presents when it's not your birthday. Today is a special day for Monica." She smiled at me.

I opened the boxes. The first one held a new hunt coat. The second one had a velvet helmet. The third one had a riding shirt and a choker pin. I had everything I needed for the Holly Hills Horse Show.

"They're beautiful," I said. "Thanks." I pretended to be really happy.

Too bad I wasn't going to ride.

* * *

After dinner, Grandpa stuck his head in my door. "Let's take Buttons for a walk," he said.

I didn't feel like it. But I knew fresh air would help. And Grandpa always knew what to say. I didn't think he could make me feel better, but I knew he'd try.

As soon as we got outside, Grandpa smiled at me. "Okay, kiddo," he said, clipping the leash around Buttons's neck. "Tell me. What's going on?"

I sighed. "I don't want to show at Holly Hills," I said. "But Mom and Logan bought me all those great riding clothes and they're so excited. So now I feel like I have to."

"They're excited because you're excited," Grandpa said. "Or I thought you were, anyway. I thought you couldn't wait to ride in a horse show. What happened? Why don't you want to ride?"

"I do want to ride in horse shows," I said. "I'm just not good enough. Trust me, that was pretty obvious today."

"How are you going to get better if you don't try?" Grandpa asked.

"I make too many mistakes," I explained. "I'll embarrass Mark and hurt his business."

Grandpa frowned at me. "All riders make mistakes," he said. "If everyone was perfect, no one would need a trainer. And that would hurt Mark's business."

He was right.

But Grandpa didn't know about Megan.

Chapter Six

Decision
Time

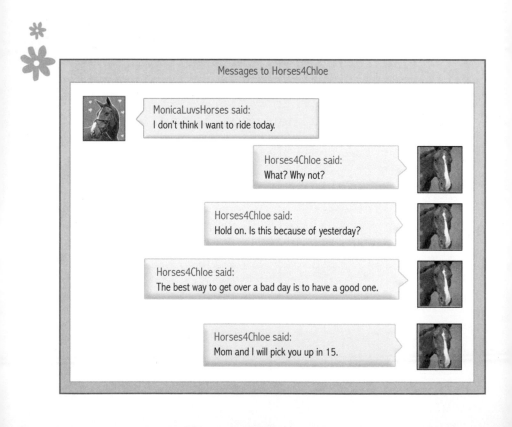

Messages to Horses4Chloe

MonicaLuvsHorses said:
I don't think I want to ride today.

Horses4Chloe said:
What? Why not?

Horses4Chloe said:
Hold on. Is this because of yesterday?

Horses4Chloe said:
The best way to get over a bad day is to have a good one.

Horses4Chloe said:
Mom and I will pick you up in 15.

The barn was deserted when Chloe and I showed up on Sunday morning. It seemed that everyone else had taken the day off, and all of the horses were resting. Rory wasn't there. Neither was Alice. Mark was in the office, doing paperwork.

"We should take it easy," Chloe said. "Let's go out on the trails."

"Lancelot will like that," I said.

Chloe and Rick-Rack led the way down the path. Lancelot didn't jiggle or pull, but I was tense. I couldn't enjoy the ride until I told Chloe what was bothering me. And I didn't really want to do that.

"What's going on?" she asked finally. I guess she could tell I was upset.

"I'm not going to show at Holly Hills," I said.

Chloe stopped and looked at me. "Monica. Are you serious?" she asked.

"Completely," I said. "I don't want to make a fool of myself again."

"You did fine for your first show," Chloe said.

"Holly Hills will be a lot harder," I pointed out. "The classes will be bigger. There will be way more people there. And my family will be there!"

"So?" Chloe said. "They'll be proud of you no matter what."

"I know," I said. "But what if I fall? I don't think I can laugh it off like Rory did."

"You're not as bad as you think, Monica," Chloe said.
She shook her head and cantered away.

I cantered after her. A huge log had fallen across the trail. Lancelot jumped it before I knew it was there.

I leaned forward without thinking and sat down gently when he landed. It was a perfect jump!

"Wow!" I said.

Chloe smiled. "See?" she said. "There's a better way to not look like a fool than giving up."

"What do you mean?" I asked.

"Become a better rider," Chloe said. "Then you have nothing to worry about."

That's when I made a decision.

I was going to train hard for the next two weeks. If I didn't feel ready on horse show day, I didn't have to enter.

Secret
Sessions

Messages to Guitar_Rory, Horses4Chloe

MonicaLuvsHorses said:
Will you guys help me train? Please?

Horses4Chloe said:
I thought you'd never ask! Definitely.

Guitar_Rory said:
I'm in. Let's start tomorrow night.

MonicaLuvsHorses said:
Thanks. I owe you both. Big time.

Rory and Chloe met me at the barn Monday evening. We had the whole place to ourselves.

"Rory and I made a schedule," Chloe said. "It covers everything that went wrong last Saturday." She showed it to me. If we did it right, we'd fix all of my problems. But I thought that was a big if.

"Let's get started," I said. "I only have two weeks till Holly Hills."

Lancelot and I walked, trotted, and cantered. We turned into the center to change direction. Then we did it ten or twelve or a million times more.

There were two jumps in the lesson ring. Rory lowered them to eighteen inches to start. On Tuesday, he raised them two inches. He did the same thing the next day.

"How high are they going to be when you're done raising them?" I asked on Wednesday.

"The real test isn't how high you can jump," Rory said.

"What is?" I asked.

"Remembering the course," Chloe explained. "That's the most important part. Don't worry about the jumps."

"I should practice the course, too," I said. "But we don't have enough jumps."

"We have enough rails," Rory said. He put some jump poles on the ground. When he was done placing them, he said, "Pretend these are fences."

Chloe drew jump-course diagrams. I had three minutes to memorize them. Then I trotted the course over the jump poles.

On Thursday, I was wrong four out of nine times. But on Friday, I got every single jump in the right order.

On Saturday morning I had my regular riding lesson.

It did not go well.

Megan and Lydia watched the whole thing, made fun of me the whole time, and I couldn't do anything right.

I missed three diagonals and a lead. Then I lost a stirrup and almost fell off.

Megan and Lydia whispered and giggled the whole time.

They weren't making it any easier for me. And I knew that was part of the problem.

I knew I'd let Megan get to me at the practice show.

But she would be at Holly Hills, too.

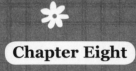
Unbeatable
Bet

Megan followed me back to the barn. I tried to ignore her but she just kept talking.

"I'm glad you didn't stop riding," Megan said. "Not everyone can win a blue ribbon in their first horse show like I did."

I tried to not roll my eyes.

"You just need more experience," Megan went on. "A lot more. No one will blame you if you don't show at Holly Hills."

"I'm riding to win at Holly Hills," I told her. Then I led Lancelot away.

I brushed Lancelot and put him in his stall. Then I took my saddle and bridle into the tack room.

I could hear voices coming from the office. Megan, Owen, and Rory were inside, talking. None of them could see me.

"She's not going to win anything at Holly Hills," Megan said.

"I think she will," Rory said. "But either way, you need to leave her alone."

"You should put your money where your mouth is," Owen said. "Why don't you guys bet on it? I'll be your witness. If Monica wins a ribbon, red or blue, Rory wins the bet. If not, Megan wins."

"I don't think so," I heard Rory say.

"I think that's a great idea," Megan said. "If you win, I'll clean the barn tack for a week."

"What if you win?" Rory asked.

All of them were quiet for a minute. Then Megan said, "If I win, you have to prep my horse for four days."

After a moment, Rory said, "Okay."

I couldn't believe it.

I left before anyone saw me. They didn't know that I knew about the bet.

I was glad Rory had faith in my skills. But now I was under even more stress. Rory would have a lot more work than Megan if he lost. I had to come in first or second in one class.

I couldn't let him down.

Chapter Nine

Still Training

When I got to the barn for training the next Friday night, Rory already had Lancelot saddled and ready to ride. Chloe wasn't there.

"Hey!" I said. "Thanks for getting Lancelot ready." Then I looked around. "Where's Chloe?" I asked. "I talked to her earlier, and she didn't tell me she was going to be late."

"She went shopping with her mom," Rory told me. "And actually, I have a lot of work to do tonight. The horses all need to be groomed and the stable has to be swept."

I frowned. "I thought we were going to train tonight," I said. "There's less than a week till the show at Holly Hills."

"Oh, you're still training," Rory said. He grinned and added, "With Mark."

"I can't afford a lesson with Mark," I said, feeling embarrassed. "Maybe I could trade two of my lessons with Alice, or something —"

But Rory cut me off. "I can't afford lessons with him either," he admitted. "But this one's free. I told Mark how Chloe and I were working with you, and he said he had some time tonight."

Just then, Mark walked out of his office. "Hi, Monica," he said. "Are you ready?"

"Yes," I said. I smiled. "Thank you so much for doing this."

Mark shrugged. "My pleasure," he said. "I've watched you ride, and I've talked to Alice about your abilities." I bit my lip, and Mark smiled. "Don't worry," he said. "You're very good. You just need a big dose of confidence."

I was so excited.

All I could do was nod.

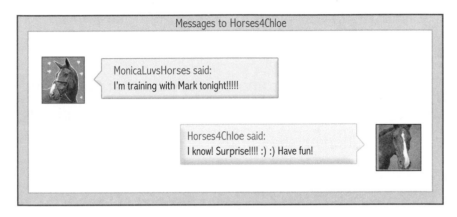

"Is it silly to want to win a blue ribbon in my first show?" I asked as we entered the ring. "Megan said she did."

"She told you that?" Mark asked. He laughed.

"Yeah. Why? Didn't she win?" I asked, frowning. It wasn't like Megan to lie.

"No, she did," Mark said. "Megan won a lead line class when she was three. She was the only kid that didn't let go of the reins or cry."

I laughed. I had pictured Megan swooping in on her horse and thrilling all the judges. All she'd done was sit on a horse.

"That is so — so — cool!" I said. I felt like a hundred pounds had been lifted off me.

While Mark and I trained, everything Rory and Chloe drilled into me clicked. I got all my diagonals and leads, and I didn't flop on the jumps.

Halfway through my lesson, I saw Rory watching. I smiled and waved. Thanks to him, I had a chance after all.

When I was done, Mark sat down with me. "That was great, Monica," he said. **"I think that your confidence is better already."**

I smiled. "I think so too," I told him. "I felt better today."

"Do you think your problems last weekend were just nerves?" Mark asked. "It was your first practice show, after all."

"I don't know," I said. I thought about Megan. I didn't want to rat her out to Mark. "I guess so."

"Well, whatever you did tonight to fix it, keep doing it," Mark said. He stood up.

"Thanks a lot, Mark," I said. "For helping me out tonight."

Mark smiled. "I didn't do anything, Monica," he said. "You did it all yourself."

Messages to Horses4Chloe

Horses4Chloe said:
Lancelot's old owner just called Mom.

MonicaLuvsHorses said:
What did she say????????

Horses4Chloe said:
She showed him for more than three years.

Horses4Chloe said:
So he's not Green. But she said he won. A lot.

MonicaLuvsHorses said:
I'm not worried about him. I'm worried about me!

I had two choices. I could ride with Chloe and Megan over higher jumps in the Junior Hunter classes. Or I could just show in the two Maiden Equitation classes.

Either way, the odds of Megan winning the bet had just gotten a lot better.

Messages to ClaudiaCristina, Artistic_Becca12

MonicaLuvsHorses said:
Can you come to my horse show?

MonicaLuvsHorses said:
It's tomorrow, in Holly Hills.

ClaudiaCristina said:
Oh no! I'd love to, but I have to babysit. Sorry!!!

Artistic_Becca12 said:
I'll see if I can find a ride. Good luck!

Chapter Ten

Rory
to the Rescue

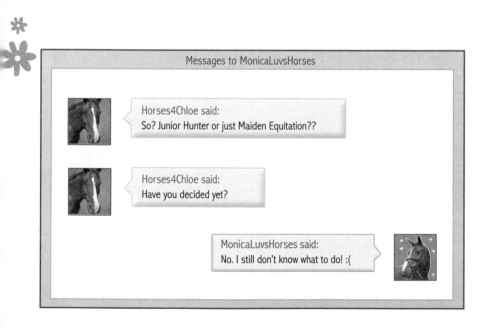

Messages to MonicaLuvsHorses

Horses4Chloe said:
So? Junior Hunter or just Maiden Equitation??

Horses4Chloe said:
Have you decided yet?

MonicaLuvsHorses said:
No. I still don't know what to do! :(

MonicaLuvsHorses said:
What should I do? Junior Hunter or just Maiden Equitation?

Guitar_Rory said:
I really don't know. I guess you kind of have to decide for yourself. But no matter what, I'll be cheering for you! Good luck today! :) :)

MonicaLuvsHorses said:
Thanks, Rory!

On Saturday morning, Grandpa drove me to Holly Hills Farm. My mom, Logan, and Angela were coming a little later.

I was wearing all of my new gear. **If I hadn't been so nervous, I would've felt great in my gorgeous new riding clothes.**

"Have you decided what to do today?" Grandpa asked as we drove. "Junior Hunter or just Maiden Equitation?"

Right then, I made up my mind.

"I'm going in the Junior Hunter classes," I said.

"Good," Grandpa said. He grinned. "You're up for the challenge."

When we pulled up to the farm, the show grounds looked like a crowded carnival. There were trucks and trailers everywhere. I didn't see the Rock Creek Stables horse van.

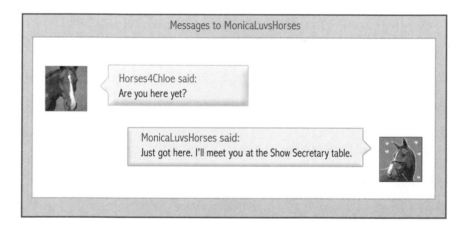

Messages to MonicaLuvsHorses

Horses4Chloe said:
Are you here yet?

MonicaLuvsHorses said:
Just got here. I'll meet you at the Show Secretary table.

Grandpa parked the car. "Good luck today, sweetheart," he said when we got out.

"Thanks, Grandpa," I said.

He gave me a great big hug. Then he left to sit in the bleachers.

I got to the Show Secretary's table just as Megan finished paying her fees. She sneered at me.

"Don't you **dare** enter Lancelot as a Green Hunter," Megan said.

"I know all about how he was shown for three years before Chloe's mom bought him."

"I'm riding him in Junior Hunter," I said.

Megan looked surprised. "Is that a good idea?" she asked, tossing her hair. "The jumps are six inches higher."

Chloe walked up and laughed. "Lancelot's last owner jumped him higher than that," she said, slinging her arm around me. "And she won blue ribbons all the time."

"That doesn't matter. Monica is the one riding him today," Megan said as she walked away.

"Ignore her," Chloe said.

"Oh, don't worry. I already am," I said, winking at my friend. "Come on. Let's get signed in."

Chloe and I filled out our forms and paid our fees. The Show Secretary gave us paper numbers to pin on our coats.

Lancelot was totally calm when I saddled him. But I wasn't. "I'm freaking out," I whispered to Chloe.

"Why?" she asked. "I mean, I know you're nervous about the show. But what exactly are you nervous about?"

"The jumps," I admitted. "They're so much higher."

"Two-foot-tall jumps and two-and-a-half-foot jumps look the same to Lancelot," Chloe said, trying to reassure me.

"The extra six inches makes a big difference to me," I said.

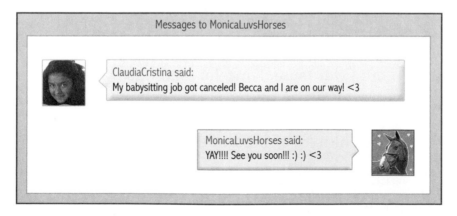

Messages to MonicaLuvsHorses

ClaudiaCristina said:
My babysitting job got canceled! Becca and I are on our way! <3

MonicaLuvsHorses said:
YAY!!!! See you soon!!! :) :) <3

Chloe brought Rick-Rack to her mom. Then she led me and Lancelot to the warm-up ring.

First I walked, trotted, and cantered. Then Chloe told me to jump the practice fence.

Rory met us there.

"That looks higher than two feet," I said.

"It's two and a half feet," Chloe said.

"You can do it," Rory added.

I stared at the fence.

I couldn't chicken out.

I had already entered the Junior Hunter over fences class.

And Megan knew it.

I cantered toward the jump. I tried to hold the reins steady, but I was tense. Lancelot didn't go over the fence. He ran around it.

I walked him for a minute. Then I tried again.

"Wait!" Rory yelled. He ran over to the jump and took off the top two rails. "Try this!"

"But that's only twelve inches high!" I said. I knew Lancelot could jump that. Easy.

"Trust me," Rory said. He waved me over the little jump.

I didn't get it, but I gave the jump a shot. Lancelot snorted as he jumped, like he was insulted.

"Do it again," Rory said.

By the time I rode around, Chloe and Rory had added a rail. Now the jump was eighteen inches high. I made that jump easily.

Then they bumped it up to two feet. I started to feel nervous, but I made it.

"Keep going!" Rory said.

I jumped the fence again.

"Two feet, three inches cleared!" Chloe exclaimed.

"And again," Rory said.

Lancelot sailed over the fence.

Two feet six inches. And I didn't flop or pull on his mouth. I did it!

Messages to GrandpaJones1945

MonicaLuvsHorses said:
I just jumped 2'6"!!!!!!!!!!

GrandpaJones1945 said:
Knew you could. Great job.

I started to relax. I had jumped the
dreaded 2'6" once. Now I knew I could jump it again.

Chapter Eleven

Show
Time

Messages to MonicaLuvsHorses

Guitar_Rory said:
One more tip. Try to forget that you're here.

MonicaLuvsHorses said:
What do you mean?

Guitar_Rory said:
Pretend like you're with Chloe and you're just having fun riding. Trust me. Pretend the judge doesn't exist.

Guitar_Rory said:
GOOD LUCK. You can do it. I believe in you!!!!

I rode Lancelot to the show ring alone.

Alice was helping the other lesson kids.

Mark and Rory were busy with the kids who owned their own horses. They always seemed to have silly last-minute problems.

Owen's boots were dusty. Lydia didn't like her hair, and Megan got hay in her lip gloss. So Rory was stuck dealing with their problems. I was sort of glad, because at least Megan wasn't following me around making me even more nervous.

Chloe was busy too. She was warming up for Advanced Equitation.

I scanned the bleachers, but I couldn't see Claudia and Becca or my mom, Logan, and Angela anywhere. There were a lot of people, though. Maybe I just couldn't find them in the crowd.

I hoped so. If I was going to do this, I needed all the support I could get.

The announcer's voice boomed through a loudspeaker. "Maiden Equitation on the flat!"

There were eighteen other riders. Everyone headed into the ring. I took a deep breath as I entered the ring. I felt calmer, and Lancelot walked without prancing.

"Trot!" the announcer said.

I remembered Rory's tip. I didn't look at the judge. I pretended I was riding with Chloe at Rock Creek. I didn't miss a diagonal, and Lancelot didn't miss a lead.

And then it was over.

I couldn't believe it. All that worrying, and it was over before I knew it.

"Walk, please, and line up!" the announcer called.

He read the names of the sixth, fifth, and fourth place winners. None of them were me.

I was disappointed. I wasn't only worried about winning the bet for Rory. I wanted a ribbon to hang in my room. Any color would have been okay with me. I decided I'd just have to try even harder in the next event.

Then the announcer said, "Third place goes to number 414, Monica Murray!"

I was thrilled.

But third place wasn't good enough to win Rory's bet with Megan.

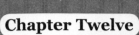
Just
Ride

Lancelot did everything right in Junior Hunter Hack. That was great. The problem was, the other horses were great, too. Ethan Westfield from Holly Hills won first place. Owen was third, and Chloe was fifth.

I didn't get anything.

I couldn't help feeling down.

"Don't be sad, Monica," Dr. Granger said afterward. "You had a great ride."

"Sometimes I don't win anything," Chloe said.

"I'm not upset for me," I said.

Chloe grinned. "Lancelot doesn't care about ribbons," she teased me.

"No, but Rory —" I stopped talking, but it was too late.

"What about Rory?" Dr. Granger asked.

Then I told them about the bet.

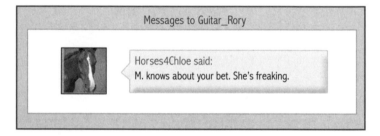

"Don't think about it," Chloe said. "Just ride."

So I did.

I was the eighth person to ride in Maiden Equitation over fences. I watched everything the first seven riders did. I even noticed some mistakes. And then I realized something. I could win red or blue if I rode perfectly.

So, of course, I blew it before the first jump. Lancelot took off on the wrong lead.

I couldn't win, but I stayed calm and started again. Lancelot didn't refuse or run out, and I didn't flop.

All the riders waited by the gate when the Show Secretary entered the ring. She handed out the ribbons. "Sixth place goes to Number 414, Monica Murray," she said.

I was stunned.

I could hardly even thank her when she gave me the green ribbon.

Grandpa, Claudia, and Becca stood up in the bleachers and cheered.

I was happy with my green sixth place. But I only had one chance left to save Rory.

I had to place first or second in Junior Hunter over fences.

Chapter Thirteen

The Winner Is

Everyone was too busy to talk before the Junior Hunter class.

Chloe and Dr. Granger were talking to Mark.

Rory was walking Merlin and Dandy.

Alice was giving the lesson kids some last-minute advice.

More advice wouldn't help me now. I knew that. I just had to ride my best, let Lancelot do his thing, and hope the judges loved my horse.

I took a deep breath.

Messages to MonicaLuvsHorses

Artistic_Becca12 said:
Here's a wave for luck! :) :) :)

I looked toward the bleachers. My family and friends did a stand-up-sit-down wave starting with Claudia and ending with Logan.

I gave them a regular wave back.

Messages to MonicaLuvsHorses

Horses4Chloe said:
Rick-Rack threw a shoe. :(

MonicaLuvsHorses said:
Oh no! Is he okay???

Horses4Chloe said:
Yeah. I think so, anyway.

Horses4Chloe said:
I can't ride him until a blacksmith fixes his shoe.

Chloe and Rick-Rack were out of the class. That meant there were twenty-one horses in the Junior Hunter over fences.

Lydia's horse bucked when she cantered her circle. Merlin moved very slowly, like he was too tired to jump. Owen had to work to keep him going. Dandy knocked down a rail, which made Megan furious.

Then it was my turn.

Lancelot broke into an easy canter and kept a steady pace. He didn't stop, run out, or pull. I didn't lose a stirrup, flop, or fall.

Every jump was perfect.

Rory rushed over when I left the ring.

"That was great!" he exclaimed. "The best in the class so far."

"I'll be happy with anything," I said.

Rory patted Lancelot's neck. "I'm sorry my bet put pressure on you, Monica. You weren't supposed to know. Megan just made me so mad."

Rory and Chloe waited with me when the winners were announced. I didn't win yellow, white, pink, or green. A Holly Hills rider came in second. I crossed my fingers, even though I was sure there was no way I could have won.

"First place goes to number 414," the Show Secretary said. "Lancelot, ridden by Monica Murray!"

Chapter Fourteen

Number
One

I gasped.

"Better get in there," Rory said, nudging me.

The next few minutes were a total blur.

I rode into the ring to get my blue ribbon. The Show Secretary put it on the bridle. Lancelot was so proud he pranced out.

All of the kids from the stable surrounded me.

"Fantastic first show, Monica!" Mark said. He smiled at me and gave me a high five. Then he handed Megan a bar of saddle soap.

Megan gasped and turned red.

Messages to MonicaLuvsHorses

GrandpaJones1945 said:
Blue Ribbon Winner gets to pick a restaurant!

GrandpaJones1945 said:
And bring your friends, too, of course.

MonicaLuvsHorses said:
Yay! Pizza Palace!!! I'll tell my friends!!! :)

I led Lancelot back to the horse van. Rory and Chloe walked with me.

"Megan is in big trouble with Mark," Chloe said.

"Why?" I asked.

"For betting against our barn," Rory explained. "Everyone from Rock Creek is on the same team."

"Lesson kids and owners," Chloe said.

"Everyone," Rory said. "Mark doesn't care if we make mistakes or come in last."

"As long as we do our best," Chloe added.

"Which I did!" I said happily.

Rory looked down. "I'm sorry I freaked you out by making that bet," he said.

"It's okay," I said. "In a way, I think it helped. I had something to ride for."

"I really did believe in you," he said, smiling at me. "I knew you could do it."

Rory grinned. Then he gave me a huge hug.

"You didn't have to win to be **number one** with me," he said.

Monica's SECRET Blog

Sunday, 4:15 p.m.

Well, it's over. My very first REAL horse show. I didn't think I'd even get one ribbon, and I ended up with three — including one BLUE ribbon!

I was so scared before the show. I'm not really sure what I was scared of. Messing up, disappointing Rory, being embarrassed in front of my friends and family. I didn't want Megan to be right. I didn't want to let Lancelot down. (I know he's a horse, but we're a team!)

I'm so glad I didn't do any of that. I'm really proud of myself. And now I have three ribbons hanging up on my bedroom wall where I can see them every day.

Okay, it wasn't the worst thing to prove Megan wrong, either. ;)

I didn't ride today. Chloe's right—nobody wants to ride the day after a show. Now I just have to figure out when I can enter the NEXT show! I hope it's soon.

In the meantime, I have a bunch of chores I didn't have time to do yesterday, so I'd better get to work!

love,

Monica

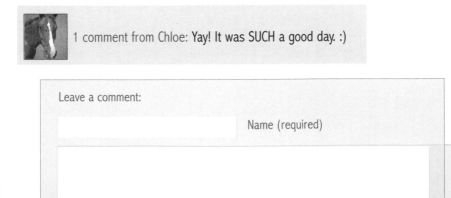

1 comment from Chloe: Yay! It was SUCH a good day. :)

Leave a comment:

Name (required)

MONICA MURRAY

▶ AVATAR

SCREEN NAME: MonicaLuvsHorses

ABOUT ME:

Activities: HORSEBACK RIDING!, hanging out with my friends, watching TV, listening to music, writing, shopping, sleeping in on weekends, swimming, watching movies . . . all the usual stuff

Favorite music: Tornado, Bad Dog, Haley Hover

Favorite books: A Tree Grows in Brooklyn, Harry Potter, Diary of Anne Frank, Phantom High

Favorite movies: Heartbreak High, Alien Hunter, Canyon Stallion

Favorite TV shows: Musical Idol, MyWorld, Boutique TV, Island

Fan of: Pine Tree Cougars, Rock Creek Stables, Pizza Palace, Red Brick Inn, K Brand Jeans, Miss Magazine, The Pinecone Press, Horse Newsletter Quarterly, Teen Scene, Boutique Magazine, Haley Hover

Groups: Peter for President!!!, Bring Back T-Shirt Tuesday, I Listen to WHCR In The Morning, Laughing Makes Everything Better!, I Have A Stepsister, Ms. Stark's Homeroom, Princess Patsy Is Annoying!, Haley Should Have Won on Musical Idol!, Pine Tree Eighth Grade, Mr. Monroe is the Best Science Teacher of All Time

Quotes: No hour of life is wasted that is spent in the saddle. ~Winston Churchill

A horse is worth more than riches. ~Spanish proverb

View Photos of Me (100)

Edit My Profile

My Friends (236)

INFORMATION:

Relationship Status:
Single

Astrological Sign:
Taurus

Current City:
Pine Tree

Family Members:
Traci Gregory
Logan Gregory
Frank Jones
Angela Gregory

Best Friends:
Claudia Cortez
Becca McDougal
Chloe Granger
Adam Locke
Rory Weber
Tommy Patterson
Peter Wiggins

Mark my words

anticipation (an-tiss-i-PAY-shuhn)—the feeling of waiting for something to happen

canter (KAN-tur)—to run at a speed between a trot and a gallop

class (KLASS)—a group

course (KORSS)—a route

diagram (DYE-uh-gram)—a drawing or plan that explains something

disqualified (diss-KWOL-uh-fyed)—prevented from taking part in an activity

equitation (eh-kwi-TAY-shuhn)—the art of horse riding

event (i-VENT)—an activity during a competition

experience (ek-SPIHR-ee-uhnss)—knowledge and skill

faith (FAYTH)—trust and confidence in someone or something

groom (GROOM)—to brush and clean an animal

mortified (MOR-ti-fyed)—very embarrassed

post (POHST)—to bob up and down in the saddle

prep (PREHP)—to get ready

stable (STAY-buhl)—a building where horses are kept

With your friends, help solve these problems.

Messages to Text 911!

1
MonicaLuvsHorses said:
How can I work on getting more confidence?

Messages to Text 911!

2
Guitar_Rory said:
How can I help my friend become braver?

Messages to Text 911!

3
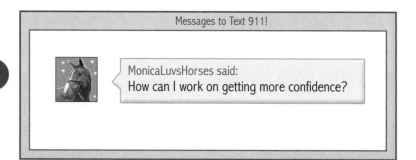

Horses4Chloe said:
Two of my friends like each other. But they're both shy. What should I do to help them?

You can write too.

Some people write in journals or diaries. I have a secret blog. Here are some writing prompts to help you write your own blog or diary entries.

1 I had an amazing time at the horse show in Holly Hills, even though I was nervous. Write about a time you were nervous but everything worked out perfectly.

2 Write about being brave. Who's the bravest person you know? Why?

3 Rory and Chloe really helped me out. How do you help your friends? How do they help you? Write about it.

ABOUT THE AUTHOR: DIANA G. GALLAGHER

Just like Monica, Diana G. Gallagher has loved riding horses since she was a little girl. And like Becca, she is an artist. Like Claudia, she often babysits little kids — usually her grandchildren. Diana has wanted to be a writer since she was twelve, and she has written dozens of books, including the Claudia Cristina Cortez series. She lives in Florida.

More stories about Best Friends

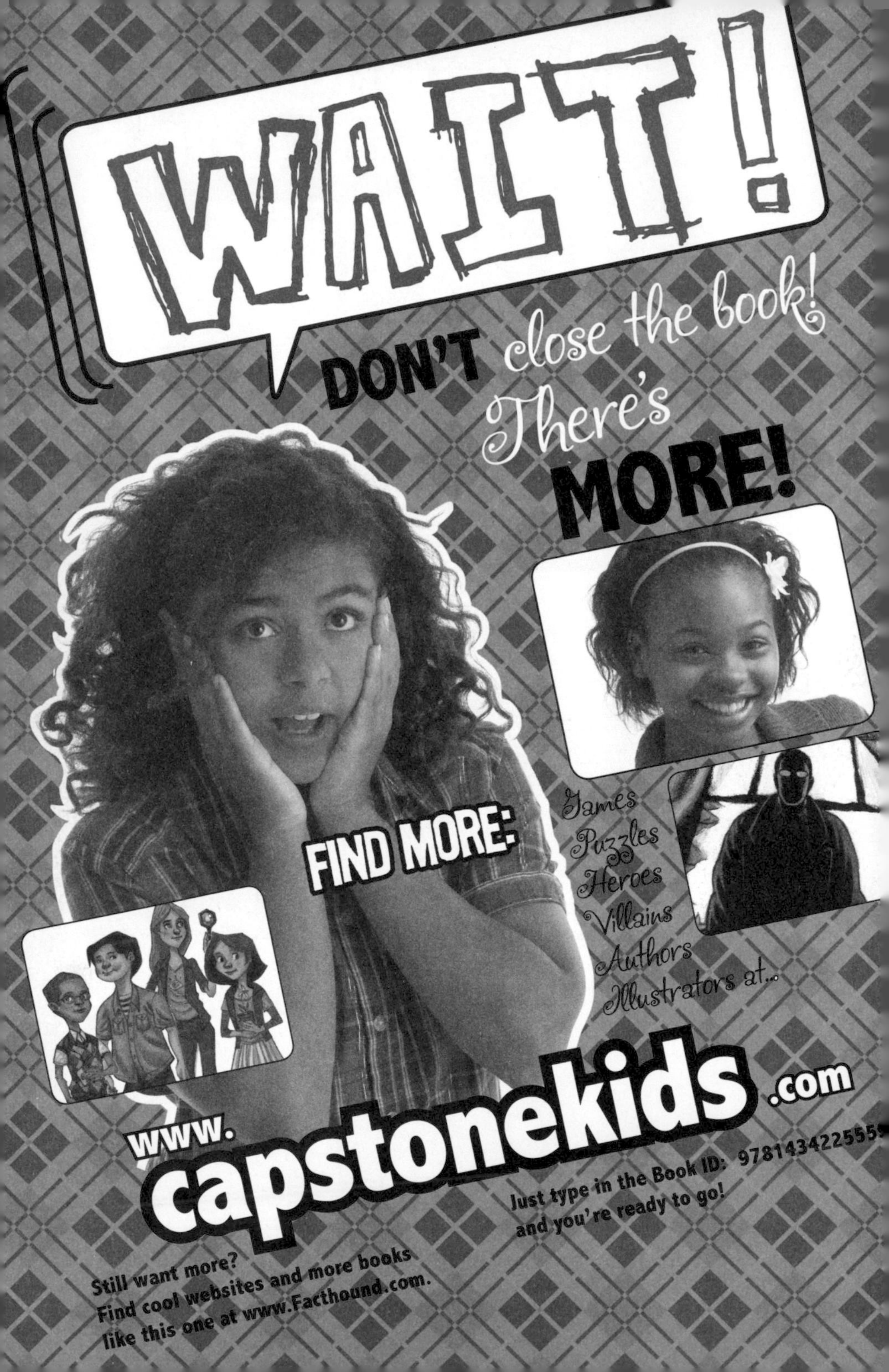
WAIT!
DON'T close the book! There's MORE!
FIND MORE:
Games
Puzzles
Heroes
Villains
Authors
Illustrators at...
www.capstonekids.com
Just type in the Book ID: 978143422555
and you're ready to go!
Still want more?
Find cool websites and more books
like this one at www.Facthound.com.